TALES FROM THE
ARABIAN NIGHTS

For Joan, Hessel,
Nicholas and Susan
G.P.

This edition first published in the United Kingdom in 2010
by Pavilion Children's Books
an imprint of Anova Books Group Ltd
10 Southcombe Street
London W14 0RA

Text copyright © 1994 Stella Maidment
Illustrations copyright © 1994 Graham Percy

A CIP catalogue record for this book is available from
the British Library.

ISBN 9781843651444

Repro by Mission Productions Ltd
Printed by Craft Print

TALES FROM THE
ARABIAN NIGHTS

Retold by
Stella Maidment

Illustrated by
Graham Percy

PAVILION
CHILDREN'S

CONTENTS

TALES FROM THE ARABIAN NIGHTS

These traditional stories have been told in the Middle East for at least a thousand years. It is said that a young woman called Scheherazade once told them to her husband, a cruel tyrant who would kill his wives when he grew tired of them. Each tale was so exciting that Scheherazade's husband couldn't wait to hear the next. Eventually he fell in love with the story-teller and gave up his wicked ways.

The first four stories in this book are about Sindbad the Sailor, a rich merchant who often sailed the seas to trade in distant lands. When he returned from his voyages Sindbad had many strange and exciting tales to tell. Here are some of his adventures, together with those of Aladdin, Ali Baba and a Persian prince and his magical Ebony Horse.

SINDBAD AND THE GIANT CLAW

Sindbad and his companions had been at sea for many weeks. They were beginning to run short of food and drink when, one morning, they came across a beautiful deserted island filled with fruit trees, flowers and sparkling streams. Thankfully they anchored the ship and went ashore.

Everyone roamed the island. After a time, Sindbad became separated from his companions. He wandered through the trees, picking the delicious fruits and marvelling at the brightly-coloured flowers. Then he sat down in the shade beside a stream and enjoyed the peace.

The next thing he knew it was late afternoon. He had slept for hours! He sprang to his feet and ran back to the shore – but where was the ship? Sindbad stared out to sea. He could just make out a tiny speck on the horizon. His ship-mates had boarded the ship and sailed away without him! No one had noticed that they had left him behind.

Sindbad felt desperate. What could he do? Was he doomed to stay alone on the island for the rest of his life? He decided to climb a tall tree and try to see if there was anything that might help him escape.

At first Sindbad could only see trees and birds, but he soon caught sight of something gleaming in the distance. It was a huge white dome, like the dome of a temple. Perhaps there were people on the island after all! He jumped down and ran through the trees to investigate.

As he got nearer, Sindbad realised that the dome was like nothing he had ever seen before. It was large and very smooth, with no windows or doors. It would have been impossible to climb and was so big that it took Sindbad fifty steps to walk all round it. Whatever could it be?

As Sindbad stood there wondering, the sky suddenly turned black. He looked up, and found himself in the shadow of a gigantic bird. The bird was flying down towards him, its huge wings blotting out the sun. Sindbad flung himself to the ground in fear. But the bird seemed not to have noticed him. It landed just beside Sindbad, on top of the giant dome. Then it fluttered its wings, made itself comfortable and promptly fell into a deep sleep.

Higher and higher it soared, taking Sindbad up into the clouds and out over the sea.

Then Sindbad remembered several stories he had heard about a gigantic bird called a roc, so huge that it fed its young on baby elephants. He realised that the white dome wasn't a building at all – it was the roc's egg! The sun had kept the egg warm all day. Now the roc had come to keep it warm through the night.

Sindbad peered up at the sleeping bird. Its huge, powerful claws were just beside him. The claws gave Sindbad an idea. Perhaps there was a way to get away from the island after all. He took off his turban, unwrapped it and twisted the cloth to make a kind of rope. Then he tied one end around his waist and the other end firmly round the bird's huge leg. The next time the roc flew off, it would take Sindbad as well!

Sindbad could hardly sleep that night for excitement. When morning came, the great bird stirred. Sindbad clung grimly to the bird's leg and hoped that his turban would not break. The roc spread its wings and rose into the air. Higher and higher it soared, taking Sindbad up into the clouds and out over the sea.

Then suddenly, the bird dropped down and landed in a rocky valley. Sindbad quickly untied his turban and jumped free. He was only just in time. The bird pounced on a snake – a huge creature as thick as a tree trunk – then flew off with the snake still wriggling in its enormous beak.

Worse still, as Sindbad looked around him, he noticed more and more gigantic snakes.

Sindbad looked around. He was in a bleak valley surrounded by huge, forbidding mountains. There seemed to be no way out. He could see no sign of water and hardly any plants. At least on the island there had been plenty to eat and drink. He began to wish he had never tried to escape. Then, as he looked down, Sindbad suddenly realised that the pieces of rock at his feet were not rock at all – they were diamonds! There were diamonds everywhere – tiny ones like pieces of gravel, and giant ones too heavy to lift. The valley was filled with riches beyond counting.

But the diamonds were of no use to Sindbad. He feared that he would never escape from the valley, and that he was doomed to starve in its scorching sun. Worse still, Sindbad began to notice more and more gigantic snakes. They were everywhere – some coiled in sleep, others crawling slowly over the ground. Sindbad was so frightened he hardly dared move.

At that moment, an extraordinary thing happened. A huge piece of raw meat came tumbling down from the mountains. It landed with a crash almost on top of Sindbad. All the snakes nearby slithered away in fright.

Sindbad stared at the meat and then looked up towards the mountain-top. He remembered a tale he had once heard about a diamond merchant who collected his stones from a valley full of snakes. The merchant threw raw meat into the valley so that the diamonds would stick to it. He waited for a vulture to pick up the meat and fly with it to a mountain ledge, then scared the vulture away and collected the diamonds embedded in the meat.

Sindbad had never quite believed that tale. Now he knew that it was true. He also saw his chance to escape. But he must act quickly! He filled his pockets with the biggest diamonds he could find. Then, using his turban once more, he tied the meat to his back, and lay face down on the ground so that it completely covered him. He did not have long to wait.

Almost immediately, a huge vulture swooped down, seized the meat in its claws, and flew with it to a ledge high on the mountain. Straight away, Sindbad heard a noise of shouting and banging. The vulture left the meat and flew away, scared by the sounds. Sindbad jumped up and began to untie himself. Just then a merchant appeared. He looked at Sindbad in great surprise and then looked down at the meat. There were no diamonds sticking to it because Sindbad had been lying underneath it.

"Don't worry, my friend," said Sindbad, "I have enough diamonds for both of us. Look! These are far bigger than the ones you would have found. Thank you for saving me!" He emptied his pockets and passed handfuls of the finest diamonds to the astonished merchant. The merchant took Sindbad to his tent and gave him some food and drink. During the meal, he listened in amazement to the story of Sindbad's adventure.

The next day the merchant took Sindbad down the mountainside and showed him the way to the nearest port. Soon Sindbad was on a ship again, his pockets filled with diamonds.

SINDBAD AND THE SAVAGE CREATURES

For a while Sindbad sailed the seas and his voyages were uneventful, but it was not long before he met with another adventure. It all began when Sindbad heard the ship's captain shouting wildly. The wind was blowing the ship off course towards a small island in the middle of the sea. "We are lost for ever!" screamed the captain. "That is the Isle of Zughb!"

Sindbad gasped. He had heard of the hordes of savage creatures who lived on the Isle of Zughb. He knew, too, that anyone who landed on the isle was never seen again.

Then Sindbad saw a crowd of strange animals racing across the beach. They were small – much smaller than Sindbad – but looked bloodthirsty and fierce. Within seconds they had plunged into the sea and were swimming out to the ship. Like a plague of insects they swarmed up the side and over the deck. There were scores of them – some climbed up the rigging, others took the wheel. The terrified crew were helpless. The creatures took over the ship, ran it aground, and forced everyone to go ashore.

"What will become of us now?" thought Sindbad. He was soon to find out. The creatures raced back to the ship and sailed away, leaving Sindbad and the other travellers stranded.

Like a plague of insects they swarmed up the side and all over the deck.

The travellers decided to search the island for shelter. They soon discovered a great palace surrounded by high walls, with an enormous black gate made of carved ebony. The gate was open. Sindbad and the others walked through it into a vast and empty courtyard. Seeing no-one, they settled down to rest in the shade.

Suddenly they heard loud, crashing footsteps. Sindbad looked up and saw a terrifying sight. A huge and hideous giant was staring down at the startled sailors.

He picked up Sindbad in his great hand and felt him all over. "Too thin!" boomed the giant, and put Sindbad down again. Then he picked up the ship's captain, who was the fattest of them all.

"That's better!" said the giant and carried him away. From the loud chomping noises coming from the palace the sailors guessed their captain's fate.

This was terrible! The island was small and there was nowhere to hide. They had no choice but to shelter in the palace walls. Yet every evening the giant would pick the fattest one of the unlucky crew and carry him off for his supper.

After several days, Sindbad and the others could stand it no longer. They thought of a daring plan to kill the giant while he was asleep. "But first," said Sindbad, "we must build a raft in case something goes wrong. If we kill the giant we can stay here until we are rescued, but if he survives we will have to try our luck at sea."

So some of the sailors built a raft from driftwood and hid it near the beach, while others carried a huge rock into the palace and positioned it carefully on a shelf near where the giant slept.

In the evening the giant came home as usual. He chose one unfortunate sailor for his supper, then fell into a deep, contented sleep. While the giant's snores echoed around the room, Sindbad and the others heaved the rock off the shelf above his head. CRASH! It hurtled down and hit the giant hard – but it did not kill him!

He staggered up, howling in pain, blood streaming into both his eyes. Now the sailors were glad of their raft! They rushed to the shore and launched it on the waves, scrambling aboard as the furious giant came lunging after them. The giant wiped his eyes, and began picking up rocks and hurling them at the terrified sailors. Many of the crew were hit – only Sindbad and two others managed to escape. They paddled furiously, until the giant was just a tiny figure in the distance and his rocks could no longer reach them.

After some time Sindbad caught sight of another island.

They managed to guide the raft on to its shores and collapsed on the beach to sleep. But Sindbad's adventures were not over yet. When he opened his eyes he saw a huge snake swallowing one of his companions whole. He woke the other sailor and they both ran for their lives. There were dangers on this island too. The next night Sindbad and his companion climbed a tree to sleep in its branches. But snakes are often good at climbing trees and again Sindbad woke to see the great snake gulping down his sleeping friend.

Now Sindbad was alone. He could hide from the snake by day but he had to sleep at night. How could he protect himself? Then he had an idea. He broke up the raft and strapped pieces

of wood all round his body until at last he was inside a large, rough wooden box. Then he fell asleep.

That night Sindbad woke to hear the snake outside. His heart began to race. Was the box strong and sharp enough to stop the snake from swallowing him? It was. The snake slithered away, disappointed, to search for other food. Sindbad was safe.

The following day, to his great joy, a ship passed by the island. Sindbad managed to signal to it and the ship altered its course and came to rescue him. When the sailors heard his tale they were all amazed. "We're heading for Baghdad now," they said. "We can take you home." Sindbad was very pleased. He did not want any more adventures, at least not for a while . . .

SINDBAD AND THE JEWELLED RIVER

One day, as Sindbad sat peacefully at home in his garden, a group of merchants came to visit him. They had just returned from a long voyage, and they told Sindbad all about their travels. When they had gone, Sindbad began to feel restless. Life in Baghdad was all very well, but he missed the excitement of travel. Within a few days, he was sailing away on a merchant ship to buy and sell fine goods in distant lands.

For many weeks all went well: the seas were calm and trade was good. But then the captain lost his way, and the ship sailed into unknown waters. Suddenly a terrible gale blew up, driving the helpless ship towards a rocky coast. The crew struggled to regain control, but it was no good. With a tremendous, splintering crash, the ship smashed against the rocks. Sindbad and the crew were thrown headlong into the huge waves, and were forced to swim for their lives.

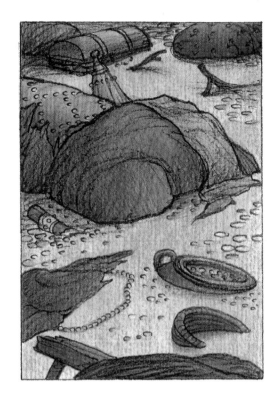

After what seemed like an eternity fighting to keep his head above the water, Sindbad was hurled onto the shore. He was the only sailor to survive.

Looking around, Sindbad realised that many other ships had suffered the same unlucky fate. Pieces of wood and shreds of sail were scattered everywhere, and other merchants' goods – including many rare and costly ornaments – rolled about across the sand. No boat could land in safety on that rocky shore.

Sindbad looked upwards. He was standing at the foot of a huge, craggy mountain, with sides far too steep to climb. He was trapped between the land and sea. Was he doomed to stay there until he starved?

Sindbad walked along the shore, looking for a way of escape. Suddenly he stopped and stared. Before him was a deep gorge at the bottom of which ran a swift-flowing river. In his travels Sindbad had seen many rivers, and each had ended its journey in the sea. Yet this one was different! As it neared the shore it turned and ran back, into a huge cave in the mountain-side.

This was strange enough, but as Sindbad drew nearer he could hardly believe his eyes. The banks of the river were covered with beautiful jewels! Rubies, emeralds, diamonds and countless other precious stones glistened and sparkled from the rocks and gleamed up from the river bed. It was a wonderful sight.

For a moment, Sindbad was transfixed by the shining brightness of the scene. Then, suddenly, he knew what he must do. He went back to the shore and collected some wooden planks, bits of rope and a few old sacks. He bound the planks together to make a raft, then scooped up handfuls of precious stones, filling each sack to the brim. He loaded the sacks onto the raft and set it on the river at the entrance to the cave. "I can't climb the mountain, but perhaps I can sail through it," thought Sindbad. "It's either that, or stay here and starve." He jumped aboard and held on tightly as the raft, swept by the fast-flowing current, sped into the darkness of the mountain.

Soon, everything went black. The huge cave narrowed to a low tunnel, and Sindbad was forced to lie flat on his face. The speed of the rushing water took his breath away, and the roaring of the river made his head throb. He lay there gasping, his heart pounding. It was far too late to turn back. He closed his eyes and fell into an exhausted sleep as the current grew faster and faster and his little raft hurtled on through the watery darkness.

When Sindbad awoke, he heard birds singing and felt the the warmth of sunshine on his skin. He sat up and looked around in bewilderment. He was in a peaceful meadow. Someone had tied his raft to the river-bank. He looked back and saw the mountain far away in the distance. He was safe! Then he heard voices. It was a group of men who had been working in the fields nearby. They had seen Sindbad's raft floating helplessly along and had caught it and tied it to a tree. Now that he was awake they gathered round, anxious to question him.

At first Sindbad couldn't understand anything they said, but then one of them spoke to him in his own language. Sindbad was overjoyed! The kind countrymen gave him food and listened as he told the story of his escape. "You must come and tell your story to our ruler, the King of Serendib," they said. They gave Sindbad a horse to ride and marched along behind him, carefully carrying his raft, still loaded with its precious cargo of jewels. Soon they came to a beautiful city in the middle of a green valley. They took Sindbad to a great palace, where the King of Serendib welcomed him and listened in amazement to his tale.

"You have suffered great hardship in our land!" he said. "You must keep the jewels as a sign of our friendship. You are welcome to stay here at the palace as my guest."

So Sindbad stayed with the king and spent many happy weeks exploring the island. At last the king asked Sindbad if he would return to his own country as a messenger to his ruler, the caliph Haroun ai-Rashid, taking him greetings and gifts.

Sindbad happily agreed to the king's request. He set sail once more, taking with him a letter and several gifts, including a wonderful cup carved from a single ruby and filled with pearls.

When at last Sindbad arrived in Baghdad he went straight to the caliph's palace and told him all that had happened. The caliph was pleased with the gifts, especially as they came from the great King of Serendib. He thanked Sindbad and gave him a generous reward. Then Sindbad returned to his family home.

"I have travelled far and seen many strange things," said Sindbad. "Now I will give up the sea and stay quietly at home with my family and friends."

SINDBAD AND THE FLYING FOLK

Sindbad stayed in Baghdad for many years. He grew older and was beginning to enjoy the comforts of a quiet life. Yet he hated to think he was too old for adventure. He decided it was time to set out on one last voyage.

After weeks of peaceful travelling Sindbad's ship sailed into a violent storm. Rain lashed down in torrents and gigantic waves tossed the ship high up in the air. Everyone was terrified. Then Sindbad saw a sight more frightening still.

Three huge whales were rushing through the waves towards

them. All were the size of mountains, and each was larger than the one before. The third whale had its mouth wide open and was just about to seize the ship between its gaping jaws.

Sindbad raced to the edge of the tilting deck and flung himself into the water. He was only just in time. Seconds later the monstrous jaws had closed and Sindbad's ship and all her crew disappeared. A stray piece of wood, flung from the deck, was all that remained of the ship. Sindbad grabbed it and used it to keep himself afloat in the stormy seas. At last, just as his strength was failing, the waves hurled Sindbad on to a deserted shore.

He staggered to his feet and looked around. He could see fruit trees and a clear running stream. At least he would be able to eat and drink!

Once he had rested and refreshed himself, Sindbad set out to find the people of that land. He walked and walked but found no sign of life. At last he came to a fast-flowing river and remembered how he had once made a raft and used it to escape through a mountain. Sindbad decided to do the same again.

He built a raft from branches tied with creeping plants, loaded it with fruit and pushed off down the river. For three days Sindbad was swept along through open, empty land.

On the fourth day he woke from sleep with a start. The raft was racing toward the top of a huge waterfall. In few seconds

Sindbad could see no way to stop the raft. There was nothing he could do but prepare for death.

he would crash over the edge and plummet to the rocks below. Sindbad could see no way to stop the raft. There was nothing he could do but prepare for death.

Just as the raft reached the very brink of the waterfall, Sindbad felt himself caught in a strong fishing net. The next thing he knew, both he and his raft were being dragged to the river bank and then out onto the land.

A group of fishermen crowded round him. They had spotted the raft on the river and had acted quickly. An old man helped Sindbad to his feet. "Come back to my house," he said. "You can rest and eat there."

The old man's house was in a nearby town. He gave Sindbad clean, new clothes to wear and sumptuous food and wine. "You can stay here as long as you like," he said kindly.

The old man and Sindbad became good friends and had many long talks together. The old man was a wealthy merchant. His wife had died, and he lived in the house with his daughter. Like Sindbad, he had once come from another land. One day the old man asked Sindbad if he would grant him a favour.

"I have no family except my one dear daughter," he said.

"I would like to see her well-married before I die. Would you take her as your wife?"

The old man's daughter was very beautiful and Sindbad was happy to agree to this request. The two were married and grew to love each other very much.

Soon afterwards, the old man died and his daughter inherited all his riches. Sindbad and his wife lived in great luxury and Sindbad looked forward to spending the rest of his life in that land. He made many new friends, but despite this still felt he was strange to them. He was anxious to find out all about their lives and customs.

It was not long before he heard of an extraordinary event that happened every year. On one particular day all the folk of the land grew wings and could fly anywhere they chose. Sindbad asked one of his new friends if he could ride on his back and so have a chance of flying too. The friend readily agreed and, when the day came, Sindbad climbed on to his friend's back and they took off – straight up into the clouds. It was a wonderful feeling!

They climbed higher and higher into the heavens. Then Sindbad began to hear the distant sound of music. It was the sweetest, most beautiful thing he had ever heard. Surely it was the sound of angels singing!

Sindbad was filled with wonder. "Glory and praise to Allah, Lord of Creation!" he exclaimed.

. . . Sindbad climbed on to his friend's back and they took off — straight into the clouds.

As soon as he uttered the words his flying friend began to lose height. It seemed as if his wings were failing him. They plummeted down on to the top of a mountain where Sindbad's friend shook him off angrily and flew away, cursing him for mentioning Allah's name.

Sindbad was mystified. Was this the way to treat a friend? And what had he done to deserve this treatment? He sat for a while alone on the mountain-top, remembering the heavenly choir and wondering why his words had made his friend so angry.

Not long afterwards Sindbad's friend returned. "I'm sorry I had to throw you off," he said. "But you mentioned the name of your god and it took away the power of my wings. In this country we never mention such things. We try never even to think of them." He let Sindbad climb on his back once more and they flew straight down to Sindbad's house.

Sindbad was very shocked by what had happened. He hurried to tell his wife. "It's true," she said. "We are living with people who know no god."

"Then we must leave at once," said Sindbad. They immediately made plans to sell their property and possessions and to take a ship back to Baghdad.

The voyage took them many weeks. At last the boat reached port. Sindbad returned to his old house and introduced his wife to his family and friends. He was relieved to have escaped the dangers of this last adventure.

Then Sindbad made a solemn vow. He promised he would never travel again – by land or sea – and he spent the rest of his life in Baghdad, living with his wife and family in peace and happiness.

ALADDIN AND THE WONDERFUL LAMP

A laddin was a young boy who lived with his mother in China long ago. His father was dead and they were very poor. One day, a wicked sorcerer came to their home. He pretended to be Aladdin's uncle, returned from abroad after many years. He said he wanted to treat Aladdin as his son and help him to become a merchant. Aladdin and his mother were delighted.

The next day, the sorcerer took Aladdin out of the city to a remote valley, far from anywhere. He built a fire, then to Aladdin's surprise began to scatter powders on the flames and chant words in an unknown language. Suddenly the ground trembled beneath their feet, then split open to reveal a dark staircase going down into the earth. Aladdin was terrified. He tried to run away, but the sorcerer held him in a fierce

grip. "Fool!" he hissed. "Don't you want to be rich?" This staircase leads to a vast treasure!"

The sorcerer had travelled many miles to reach this place. He knew that a powerful magic lamp was buried there, but he could not get the lamp himself. Only young Aladdin could enter the secret cave.

He told Aladdin what to do. "Go down the staircase. At the bottom you will find three caves, each filled with jars of gold. Don't touch the jars – go on into a walled garden. There's an old lamp standing in a niche in the wall. Bring me the lamp, and we will both be rich!"

Secretly, the sorcerer was planning to grab the magic lamp and leave Aladdin in the cave. Seeing Aladdin hesitate, he pulled a ring off his own hand. "Wear this magic ring," he said. "It will guard you from harm. Now go!"

Inside the cave, everything was just as the sorcerer had described, but Aladdin was amazed by the beauty of the garden. It was filled with trees covered in brightly coloured fruits. Each one was made from a precious stone, and every single fruit was worth a fortune.

Aladdin found the old lamp and pushed it into his shirt. Then he set about collecting some of the fruits before he left the cave. As he climbed back up the stairs, he saw his uncle's

There was a flash of light, and a strange figure appeared in the air.

face peering down. "Give me the lamp!" the sorcerer whispered, stretching out his hand.

"My hands are full," Aladdin said. "Help me out first, and then I'll give it to you."

"GIVE ME THE LAMP!" roared the sorcerer. He looked so fierce that Aladdin staggered back in fear. The sorcerer thought that Aladdin meant to keep the lamp for himself. He spread his arms and chanted more strange words. With a great, rumbling crash, the earth closed once more over the entrance to the stairs.

Now Aladdin was truly terrified. He paced up and down, wringing his hands in despair. As he did this, he accidentally rubbed the magic ring. There was a flash of light and a strange figure appeared in the air. "I am the genie of the ring!" it said. "What do you want, oh master?"

For a moment Aladdin was speechless with surprise. Then he said, "I want to get out of this cave!" Suddenly, he found himself standing on the grass outside. The sorcerer was nowhere to be seen.

Aladdin returned home and told his mother what had happened. The next day, they decided to sell the old lamp at the market so they could buy some bread. "Let me clean it first," said his mother, and started to rub the lamp with a cloth.

With the genie's help, Aladdin built a wonderful new palace . . .

Suddenly, there was flash of light and a huge genie appeared. "I am the genie of the lamp!" it roared. "What do you want, oh mistress?"

The poor woman was so startled that she fell into a faint, but Aladdin spoke quickly. "She wants you to bring us some food!" he said. Instantly, a delicious feast appeared, arranged on twelve huge golden plates. Aladdin realised that they would never be hungry again.

After that, whenever Aladdin needed money he sold one of the gold plates. In this way, he and his mother lived comfortably for several years. Then, one day, Aladdin caught a glimpse of the king's young daughter as she rode through the town. He fell in love with her at once, and longed to marry her.

He took the last gold plate and loaded it with the fruits he had brought from the cave. His mother took it to the King. The king was so impressed by the wonderful jewels that he agreed to let Aladdin marry his daughter.

With the genie's help, Aladdin built a wonderful new palace beside the king's old one. There he and his bride lived happily together, with the lamp standing in a place of honour in Aladdin's private room.

It was not long before all their happiness was shattered. The sorcerer heard about the marriage and realised that Aladdin

must have escaped. He decided to try once more to get the magic lamp. He came to the palace dressed as a peddler carrying a basket of polished lamps. "New lamps for old! New lamps for old!" he called. The people in the street began to laugh. The peddler must be mad!

The princess and her maid heard the commotion. The maid asked if she could take the old lamp from Aladdin's room and change it for a new one. Aladdin was out hunting and the princess, who did not know the lamp's secret, laughingly agreed.

As soon as the sorcerer saw the lamp, he grabbed it, threw down his basket and ran off. The crowd laughed even more. But no-one laughed a minute later, when Aladdin's palace and everyone in it vanished. The sorcerer had used the lamp to take himself and the palace to Morocco, thousands of miles away.

When Aladdin found out what had happened, he was horrified. He began to search all over the land for his beloved wife. After many days he sat by a river in deep despair.

He washed his hands in the cool water and accidentally rubbed the magic ring. The genie instantly appeared.

"I am the genie of the ring. What do you want, oh master?" "Bring back my palace!" said Aladdin.

"I'm sorry, master, that I cannot do."

"Then take me to my wife!" said Aladdin.

Straight away he found himself in his palace in the sorcerer's land. The princess flung herself into Aladdin's arms and told him what had happened. The sorcerer had sworn that Aladdin was dead. He wanted the princess to marry him instead – and he carried the lamp with him everywhere he went!

Aladdin rubbed the ring again and asked the genie for a sleeping powder. They mixed it in a cup of wine. Then Aladdin hid behind a screen. When the sorcerer returned, he found the princess smiling. She offered him the drugged wine, which he drank greedily. Then he fell to the ground in a deep sleep.

Aladdin leaped out and seized the lamp from the sorcerer's clothes. He threw the sorcerer out of the window, rubbed the lamp and asked the genie to take the palace back to China.

Once more Aladdin's palace stood beside the king's. And from that day on, Aladdin and his beloved wife lived happily ever after.

THE EBONY HORSE

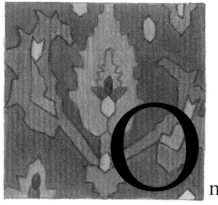

Once there was a king of Persia who loved new inventions. Every feast day, he asked his subjects to bring him any unusual new machines. He would give a prize to those he liked the best.

On one important feast day the king announced that there were to be three very special prizes. The inventors of the three best machines would each be allowed to marry one of the king's three daughters. That day three inventors came to the court. Two were clever young men and one was a wicked sorcerer. The first inventor brought a carved peacock. "This bird will tell the time," he said. "Wind it up and it will flap its wings and make a sound on every hour." The young man gave a demonstration. The king was much amused, and offered the hand of his eldest daughter in marriage.

The second inventor brought a golden trumpet. "Place this above your palace gate," he said, "and it will sound when any enemy approaches." The inventor showed how the trumpet worked and the king was thrilled with his idea. He offered the second inventor the hand of his middle daughter in marriage.

Then it was the turn of the third inventor, the ugly old sorcerer. When he revealed his creation the court gasped in astonishment. It was the most beautiful horse that anyone had ever seen, carved from solid ebony, with eyes of diamonds and a mane and tail of finest silk. It was as life-like as any

horse in the king's stables. "But that's not all!" boasted the sorcerer. "This horse will take you anywhere you want to go!"

The king's young son begged to be the first to try it out. He climbed into the saddle, and the sorcerer began to explain the controls. "There's a switch here," he said, "which starts everything going . . ." Then the sorcerer accidentally turned the switch. Suddenly the horse rose up into the air and began to flyaway.

Everyone gasped – the horse was more marvellous than anything they had ever expected. But where was it taking their handsome young prince?

The prince held on tightly as the ebony horse flew higher and higher. He had no idea how to stop it, but he kept calm and began to search for any other controls. He found two more switches underneath the horse's mane. One made the horse fly higher and faster, the other made it fly lower and slower. Now the prince could enjoy his flight, knowing that he could land in safety. He flew for miles that day, over many foreign lands. At last, as it was growing dark, he decided to stop for the night. He saw a stately palace on the edge of a city and guided the horse to land upon its roof.

The prince crept down through the palace. Everything seemed very quiet. Then he heard the sound of laughter and women's voices. He walked into a room, and came face to face with the most beautiful young woman he had ever seen. The prince did not know that the woman was the daughter of the king of this foreign land. The palace had been built specially for her.

At first the princess was alarmed to find a strange young man in her palace, but his manners were so graceful that she was quickly reassured. After the prince had told her his story, she sent for food and drink and ordered a room to be prepared where he could rest for the night.

The next morning, the prince found the princess looking sad. "You must go now," she said. "My father will kill you if he finds you here. He will never believe the story of your flying horse, and will think you are a common thief. Besides," she said,

He saw a stately palace on the edge of the city, and guided the horse to land upon its roof.

looking even more sad, "he has arranged for me to be married today, to a distant cousin who is old and rich."

The prince begged the princess to come back with him to Persia as his bride. She loved him just as he loved her and happily agreed. They crept onto the palace roof, climbed on the horse's back and flew up into the morning sky.

As they flew over Persia the prince decided that his princess must be welcomed in the proper way. He stopped in a garden just outside the city and left the princess with the horse while he rushed to tell his father the good news and to arrange a royal procession to carry his bride through the city streets.

But in the long hours that had passed, the king had given up his son for lost. Instead of rewarding the sorcerer for his clever invention, the king had punished him. The sorcerer was whipped and sent away, lucky to have escaped with his life. Now he was anxious to find his ebony horse and take his revenge. He had watched and waited for the prince's return, and was the only person to see the prince and princess gliding down to earth.

While the prince was away, the sorcerer hurried into the garden. He told the princess that he had come to take her to the court. She was surprised, but since the old man clearly knew how to work the flying horse, she agreed to climb up behind him.

As they flew towards the court, the princess saw the prince, his father and a procession of courtiers riding out to meet her. The sorcerer laughed. "Let them see who won the prize!" he boasted, swooping down low so that everyone saw the beautiful princess. Then, he changed the controls and the horse flew up and away. Many hours later, the sorcerer stopped the horse in a field. The princess leaped off.

"Where have you taken me?" she cried.

"Far, far away!" laughed the wicked man. "And now I have my revenge. I had hoped to marry the King of Persia's daughter, but one princess is much like another. I shall marry you instead." At these words, the princess began to cry.

It so happened that the king of that distant land was riding by. He saw the old man and the weeping girl and asked them what was going on. "She is my wife!" said the sorcerer. "Mind your own business!" But the princess begged the king to help her, saying she was nothing of the sort. The king believed her.

He sent the wicked sorcerer to prison and took the princess to his palace. He, too, had fallen in love with her and hoped that one day, she might be his wife.

Meanwhile, the Prince of Persia was distraught. He rode all over the land and far beyond it, searching desperately for his dear princess. At last, after many days of travelling, he heard some news. He heard that the sorcerer was in prison, and that the princess was living in the court of a foreign king who wanted to marry her. But he also heard that the princess had turned quite mad, and seemed possessed by evil spirits.

The prince guessed rightly that the madness was only an act. It was the princess's clever way of preventing the marriage until she could escape.

Then the prince thought of a plan to rescue the princess. He travelled to the foreign king's court and announced that he was a magical doctor specialising in diseases of the brain. He claimed that he could cure those possessed by evil spirits. "You are more than welcome," said the king. "Perhaps you can cure the poor young woman who rants and raves upstairs."

He led the prince to the princess's room. The prince pretended to recite magical chants, but in between the words he whispered to the princess, "Pretend to be better, but not completely well.

Tomorrow we will go!" The princess did as he said, behaving more calmly but still seeming slightly strange. Then the prince spoke to the king. "This madness comes from the ebony horse," he declared, "but the horse may cure it, too. Tomorrow morning, take the young woman and the horse back to the field where you found them. Keep well back, for my spells are dangerous. After that, all will be well."

The next day, the king and all his court stood at a safe distance as the prince lit fires in a circle around the horse so that the smoke concealed it. He and the princess climbed on to the horse's back and in a moment they had flown away.

There was great celebration when the two returned. They were married immediately, and the princess wrote to her father telling him that she had married the King of Persia's son. Her father was delighted, and gave them his blessing. In due course the prince inherited his father's kingdom and he and his wife lived happily ever after.

As for the ebony horse – it stayed in the palace looking as beautiful as ever. But the wise old King of Persia took its switches out and threw them away. It never flew again.

ALI BABA AND THE FORTY THIEVES

Long ago in Persia, there lived two brothers called Kasim and Ali Baba. Kasim, the elder, was very rich and greedy. Ali Baba, on the other hand, was poor but generous. He was only a humble woodcutter but he never complained, nor envied his brother's wealth.

One day, when Ali Baba was in the forest, he heard the sound of galloping hooves. He peered through the trees and saw a band of forty evil-looking men, each carrying a heavy saddlebag. Ali Baba guessed that they were thieves.

The men stopped by a large rock in the hillside. Their leader shouted "Open Sesame!" To Ali Baba's astonishment the rock began to move, revealing an opening into the hill. The thieves dismounted and carried their saddlebags into the cave.

Soon afterwards the men appeared again, empty-handed. They climbed onto their horses, and their leader turned and shouted "Close Sesame!" Within seconds the doorway in the rock had closed, and the men had galloped away.

Ali Baba crept down to the rock. Standing in front of it, he whispered "Open Sesame!" Just as before, the rock split open and the doorway appeared. Ali Baba tiptoed into a huge cavern.

There was treasure everywhere: glittering jewels, gold and silver coins, bales of brightly-coloured silk and hundreds of costly ornaments. Many of the bags were overflowing, and coins and precious stones spilt out upon the floor. The cave must have been used by thieves as a hiding place for many years.

Ali Baba took three sacks and filled each one with golden coins, gathering them up from the overflowing treasure on the floor so the robbers would not notice they had gone. "This will be more than enough for me," he thought. As he left the cave, he turned back to the door and whispered the words "Close Sesame!" The rock obeyed, and all was as before.

Ali Baba hurried home to tell his wife the news. "We must spend the money carefully," he said, "so that no-one notices how rich we are. If the robbers hear about our wealth, they may guess that I have discovered their secret."

But Ali Baba's brother noticed the change in their fortunes straight away. "Where has all this money come from?" he asked, accusingly. Ali Baba felt sure that he could trust his own brother, so he told Kasim the whole story. He thought his brother would be glad for him, but greedy Kasim was only thinking of himself. The next day Kasim took ten large bags and set off for the forest. "This will be the first of many trips!" he chuckled. He found the rock that Ali Baba had described. "Open Sesame!" he shouted and marched inside. Then he shouted "Close Sesame!" in case anyone saw that the doorway was open.

Kasim took a long time to load his ten bags. He kept stopping and wondering which objects were the most valuable. At last he stood in front of the closed doorway ready to say the magic words. But what were they? He knew they were something to do with grain. "Open Barley!" he shouted; "Open Corn!" But nothing happened. Try as he might, Kasim could not remember the correct words.

After a while, he heard the sound of horses outside. The robbers had returned. A voice cried, "Open Sesame!" and, too late, Kasim remembered what he should have said. The robbers seized him and fell upon him swiftly with their swords.

The next day Kasim's wife went to Ali Baba's house in tears. "Kasim went to the cave yesterday," she said. "He was going to bring back ten bags of treasure, but he hasn't come back at all!"

Ali Baba hurried to the cave. He went inside and found his brother's body lying by the door. With great sadness Ali Baba carried the body home to be buried.

A week later the robbers came back to the cave. When they saw that Kasim's body had disappeared they realised that someone else must know their secret. They hurried to the nearby town to find out who had died recently and who their closest relative was. The thieves soon learned of Kasim's death and heard that Kasim's wife was staying at the house of his brother, Ali Baba.

One evening soon after, the robbers' leader came to Ali Baba's house with a cart containing forty huge oil jars. "I am a humble oil merchant," he said. "I need a place to rest. Would you be kind enough to let me stay?"

Ali Baba agreed without a second thought. He didn't know that only one of the jars was filled with oil. In each of the other thirty-nine jars crouched a robber armed with a dagger and a knife. "Wait for the sign!" muttered the robber chief to the jars. "Then kill everyone in the house!"

He followed Ali Baba inside, and joined the family for supper . . .

54

He followed Ali Baba inside, and joined the family for supper, behaving all the time like a well-mannered guest.

That night, when Ali Baba's servant girl, Marjanah, was washing the dishes, she noticed that her lamp had almost run out of oil. She remembered the huge jars outside. "I'm sure the merchant wouldn't mind if I took just a little oil for my lamp," she thought. Just as she touched the lid of the first jar, she heard a muffled voice coming from inside it. "Is it time to kill them?" said the voice.

Marjanah was astonished and frightened too – but she didn't scream or run away. She thought quickly and replied, in as calm a voice as she could manage, "Not yet, later!"

Then she walked up to the second jar. The same thing happened. Another muffled voice said, "Is it time to kill them?" Marjanah was beginning to understand what was going on. "Not yet, later," she said, and walked on to the next jar.

Finally Marjanah reached the fortieth jar. No-one spoke. She lifted the lid and found that it was full of oil. Thoughts were racing through her head. There were thirty-nine villains waiting to set upon the house – and perhaps another villain tucked away inside. Ali Baba's household was no match for such a horde. How could she save them all?

Then Marjanah knew what she must do. She took the oil from the last great jar and slowly heated it in her cooking pot. Then, trembling with fear, she carried the pot outside and poured boiling oil into each of the jars. One by one, she killed all of the thirty-nine thieves.

At midnight the robber chief leant out of his window. "It's time!" he called softly, "You can come out!" But there was no

answer. He called louder, but still there was no reply. Finally, he came downstairs. When he saw what had happened he was filled with fear. He leaped over the wall and ran away. Marjanah watched him leave. She had stayed up in the dark kitchen until she could be sure that the household was safe once more.

The next day, Marjanah told Ali Baba everything. He was filled with gratitude for the loyal servant girl. "From now on," he said, "I consider you my daughter, not my servant."

But this was not the end of the story. Many months later, Ali Baba's grown-up son asked if he could invite a friend to dine with them. Ali Baba readily agreed, and that evening an old man with a long white beard arrived.

There was much merriment in the house that night but young Marjanah did not smile. Her sharp eyes had recognised the face behind the long white beard. She felt sure it was the robbers' leader in disguise. As she looked closely at the man, she noticed something gleaming in the folds of his sleeve. It was a knife! Now she was sure. He had returned to kill them all.

Luckily for Ali Baba, Marjanah was as clever as she was beautiful. She went upstairs and dressed in dancing clothes,

including a golden belt with a jade-handled dagger hanging from it. Then she began to dance, to entertain the guest.

Marjanah danced beautifully and everyone was entranced. Even the robber chief smiled and clapped as she began the traditional dagger dance swaying to the music and waving her dagger gracefully in the air. Slowly

Marjanah danced beautifully, and everyone was entranced.

Marjanah danced towards the wicked man. Then, before anyone could stop her, she pounced on him and stabbed him through the heart.

"Marjanah! Are you mad? What have you done?" cried Ali Baba. Marjanah did not need to answer. The false white beard had slipped, revealing the cruel robber's face, while at the same time the knife fell from his sleeve and clattered to the floor.

Ali Baba was overwhelmed with gratitude. "Without you, we would all be dead," he said. "Will you do me the honour of marrying my son and so truly become part of my family?"

Marjanah had long admired Ali Baba's son, and he in turn was pleased to have a wife so clever and so brave. From that day on, the family lived in happiness and peace.